Patagonia Clatterbottom is the head teacher of Pirate School.

Today she's going to teach Smudge, Flo, Ziggy and Corkella . . .

. . . how to make a proper pirate attack!

Jeremy Strong once worked in a bakery, putting the jam into three thousand doughnuts every night. Now he puts the jam in stories instead, which he finds much more exciting. At the age of three, he fell out of a first-floor bedroom window and landed on his head. His mother says that this damaged him for the rest of his life and refuses to take any responsibility. He loves writing stories because he says it is 'the only time you alone have complete control and can make anything happen'. His ambition is to make you laugh (or at least snuffle). Jeremy Strong lives near Bath with four cats and a flying cow.

Books by Jeremy Strong

**GIANT JIM AND THE HURRICANE
THE INDOOR PIRATES
THE INDOOR PIRATES ON TREASURE ISLAND
MY BROTHER'S FAMOUS BOTTOM
MY DAD'S GOT AN ALLIGATOR!
MY GRANNY'S GREAT ESCAPE
MY MUM'S GOING TO EXPLODE!
THERE'S A PHARAOH IN OUR BATH!**

**PIRATE SCHOOL – JUST A BIT OF WIND
PIRATE SCHOOL – THE BIRTHDAY BASH
PIRATE SCHOOL – WHERE'S THAT DOG?
PIRATE SCHOOL – THE BUN GUN
PIRATE SCHOOL – A VERY FISHY BATTLE**

Jeremy Strong
Pirate School

A
Very
Fishy
Battle

Illustrated by Ian Cunliffe

PUFFIN

This is for Sam and small pirates everywhere

PUFFIN BOOKS

Published by the Penguin Group
Penguin Books Ltd, 80 Strand, London WC2R 0RL, England
Penguin Group (USA) Inc., 375 Hudson Street, New York, New York 10014, USA
Penguin Group (Canada), 90 Eglinton Avenue East, Suite 700, Toronto, Ontario, Canada M4P 2Y3
(a division of Pearson Penguin Canada Inc.)
Penguin Ireland, 25 St Stephen's Green, Dublin 2, Ireland (a division of Penguin Books Ltd)
Penguin Group (Australia), 250 Camberwell Road, Camberwell, Victoria 3124, Australia
(a division of Pearson Australia Group Pty Ltd)
Penguin Books India Pvt Ltd, 11 Community Centre, Panchsheel Park, New Delhi – 110 017, India
Penguin Group (NZ), 67 Apollo Drive, Rosedale, North Shore 0632, New Zealand
(a division of Pearson New Zealand Ltd)
Penguin Books (South Africa) (Pty) Ltd, 24 Sturdee Avenue, Rosebank, Johannesburg 2196, South Africa

Penguin Books Ltd, Registered Offices: 80 Strand, London WC2R 0RL, England

puffinbooks.com

First published 2007
4

Text copyright © Jeremy Strong, 2007
Illustrations copyright © Ian Cunliffe, 2007
All rights reserved

The moral right of the author and illustrator has been asserted

Set in Times New Roman
Made and printed in Singapore by Star Standard

British Library Cataloguing in Publication Data
A CIP catalogue record for this book is available from the British Library

ISBN: 978–0–141–32096–0

Contents

1. Let's Attack the Woppagobs!

It was another sunny day at Pirate School.

Corkella was having a lot of fun swimming with the local dolphins. She was pretending they were in her school and she was in charge.

"I'm the fiercest head teacher in the world," said Corkella, trying to look scary. "Stand on your tails!"

A loud bellow thundered over the waves. "Who says they're the fiercest head teacher? I'm the fiercest head teacher! How dare you!" It was Patagonia Clatterbottom herself, the

real head of Pirate School, and a
nightmare on legs. She looked angry
enough to burst into flames.

FWOOOSH! Patagonia pulled
off her wooden leg and hurled it at
Corkella. Fortunately it missed by
miles. One of the dolphins batted it
straight back at her with his tail.

The head yelled at Corkella. "Get back on deck at once. I have an important announcement. Miss Snitty, push me on to the poop deck."

Miss Snitty was as thin as a piece of string and just as loopy. She was the school secretary, but spent most of her time pushing the head about in her boat-pram.

The boat-pram had an anchor, two sails, three flags and four cannons. BOOM! That was one going off. Patagonia liked to make as much noise as possible.

"Is everybody here?" bellowed the head teacher. "What's wrong with your teeth, Ziggy? Have they grown?"

Ziggy's teeth seemed to be twice their normal size and stuck out of his mouth.

"I think they're falling out –" he began and all at once the fangs shot from his mouth and fastened on to the end of Patagonia's enormous nose.

"Aargh! Get 'em off me! You horrible child! You and your jokes!" She threw the teeth back at him. "I shall have you scrumbled!"

The children looked at each other.
Scrumbled? What did that mean?

"I think it's like being scrambled,"
Smudge whispered to Little Flo, "but
worse." Little Flo turned pale.

"You useless lot of lily-livered
lollipops," shouted Patagonia.

"Today you are going to learn how to make a proper pirate attack. We are going to set sail and attack the Woppagobs on Woppagob Island!"

A gasp came from the children. A real pirate attack! On the Woppagobs!

2. The Crisps Get Kidnapped

“First of all we need lots of supplies,” ordered Patagonia. “Smudge and Miss Fishgripp can go to the supermarket for us. Here’s my list.”

Shopping List for Attack
on Woppagobs

20 tins sardines (1 tin each, plus
11 extra for Mrs P. Clatterbottom)

100 packets of crisps (1 packet
each, plus 91 extra for Mrs P.
Clatterbottom)

10 cannonballs (large)
15 cannonballs (medium)
20 cannonballs (small)

3 coils of rope (for tying up
Woppagobs)

1 giant pack of assorted bandages
and eyepatches

"I hope we won't need the bandages," murmured Smudge, as they trailed around the supermarket.

"Don't you worry, laddie," growled Miss Fishgripp, who taught hand-to-hand fighting and wore a belt with fifteen swords stuck into it. "I shall protect everyone."

But when they got back to the harbour, disaster struck.

RAAAARGH!!

An ambush! The Woppagobs! They

threw themselves on Smudge and Miss Fishgripp.

"Don't be scared!" yelled Miss Fishgripp. "I shall turn them into mincemeat!" She whipped out two of her swords, slicing right through her belt. Her trousers fell down around her ankles. Smudge sighed. That was what happened EVERY TIME!

"Piddly-poos! Look at spotty knicky-knoos!" laughed the chief Woppagob, Boris Bigbelly. They grabbed all the food (but left the cannonballs and rope and bandages), tumbled into their boat and departed at high speed, singing.

When Patagonia heard what had
happened she almost exploded on
the spot. "I thought you were good
at fighting!" she snapped at Miss
Fishgripp.

"I am," insisted the teacher. "But I'm
at my best when my trousers are up."

"Those Woppagobs are always after
our food," Patagonia raged. "And this
time they've kidnapped my crisps.
We shall have to rescue them. Set sail
at once! Belay the cranking irons!
Splinkle my tagglepins!"

The wind filled the sails and the ship sailed out to sea, followed by Corkella's fleet of dolphins.

"They understand everything I say," smiled Corkella.

"Stupid girl," muttered the head teacher. "You can't be friends with dolphins. They're fish."

"No, they're mammals," corrected Ziggy.

"Grrrrrr! I'll have your head chopped off for arguing," said Patagonia.

"They'll still be mammals," Ziggy pointed out, baring his joke teeth. Patagonia took a step back, rubbed her nose thoughtfully and scowled.

3. A Deadly Trick

On Woppagob Island, the Woppagob gang were having a fine old time. They danced around their campfire, singing and shouting.

"Did you see me poke Fishgripp in the eye?" claimed Fifi Foh-Fum.

"No," chorused the other three.

"Did you see ME push Smudge off a cliff?" boasted Two-Tooth Charlie.

"No," said the others.

"It doesn't matter who did what," yelled Boris Bigbelly. "We got their food! Who wants a sardine?"

Everyone wanted a sardine, but none of them could work out how to open the tin. Lily Lollop reckoned you had to push the lid very hard, so she did.

A squirt of oil shot straight into Boris's eye and a sardine got stuck up his nose, head first.

He chased Lily halfway around the island, pelting her with sardines.

And when they reached the other side they saw a pirate ship coming towards them.

"It's Fattybonio Splatterbottom and her tiddly-diddly pirates," muttered Boris. "It looks like they're going to attack. Quick, back to camp."

"I expect they are planning to surprise us," Boris told the gang. "But we are going to surprise them."

"How?" asked Two-Tooth Charlie.

Boris Bigbelly grinned. "When they get here, we shall all be dead."

"I don't want to be dead!" wailed Lily.

"Stop blubbing! We won't really be dead. That's the surprise. We pretend to be dead and when those stupid pirates come close enough we jump up and get them."

The others stared at Boris in
amazement. How did he get such
clever ideas? Boris tucked into a tin
of sardines. "I eat lots of fish," he told
them. "It makes you clever."

"Is that why there's a sardine up your
nose?" asked Fifi innocently. Boris
pretended that he had meant to put it
there.

"It's the latest fashion," he claimed. "Ordinary people have rings and studs in their noses, but I have a sardine, and that makes me VERY special."

"It certainly does," agreed Fifi, giving the others a sly grin.

Just then there was a loud bang, followed by a whistling noise.

"Duck!" yelled Boris.

"That's not a duck, it's a cannonball," said Two-Tooth Charlie.

He pointed at the ball as it went
whizzing over their heads and crashed
into the trees. A bird came squawking
out, with all its tail feathers missing.
"That's a duck," Charlie said.

"An unlucky ducky," added Lily.

The Woppagobs left the crisps and
sardines piled up on the beach and took
cover in their nearby cave while more
cannonballs crashed around them.

"We shall hide here until they reach the shore. Then we'll lie down on the sand and pretend to be dead," said Boris.

"Won't the pirates be surprised!" chuckled Fifi.

"Dead surprised!" sniggered Lily.

4. Patagonia's Plan

Patagonia Clatterbottom's first plan of attack was simple. She wanted to blow up the Woppagobs with cannonballs. But Smudge had a better idea.

"We should capture them," he said. "Then we can rescue the crisps and sardines."

"Woof," said Jazz, the ship's dog, which meant that she agreed.

"What's the point of being captain if you won't take my orders?" growled Patagonia. "Right, this is plan two. We anchor in the bay. You children keep firing the cannons. I will lead the staff ashore in the rowing boat. We'll creep up on the Woppagobs and capture them."

They all agreed that was a better idea, even though Ziggy wanted to go ashore and have a proper sword fight.

Mad Maggott, Miss Fishgripp, Mrs Muggwump, Miss Snitty and Patagonia clambered into the rowing boat while the children started firing the cannons. The little boat had almost reached land when there was an unfortunate accident. Jazz got rather overexcited and jumped on a cannon just as it was firing. BANG!!

The barrel tipped up. The cannonball went up into the sky, higher and higher. It stopped. It came back down, faster and faster, until KERRUNCH! It plunged straight through the bottom of the little rowing boat.

"Oops!" grinned Ziggy.

Patagonia and the staff were hurled into the sea. "Those stupid kids have blown us up!" roared Patagonia. "Snitty! Carry me to the beach!"

They splashed ashore at last.

"Good, now we shall creep up on the Woppagobs and give them a nasty shock," growled Patagonia. "Follow me, and keep quiet."

At that moment another cannonball screamed overhead and scored a direct hit on the pile of crisps. The bags burst and thousands of crisps came floating down like snow, covering the island.

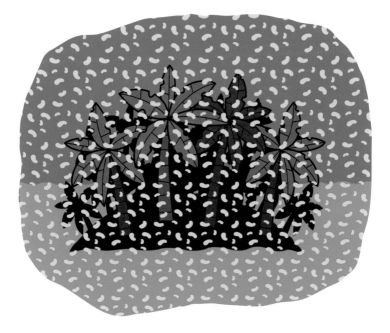

"Spanking spiggots!" hissed Patagonia. "First of all those kids blow up my boat and now they've blown up my crisps! The island is covered in them. We can't possibly creep around silently now. Grrrrr!"

"It's all right," cried Mad Maggott, peering round a rock. "Look – all the Woppagobs are dead!"

"We've won!" yelled Patagonia triumphantly.

"No you haven't!" bellowed the Woppagobs, jumping to their feet. In a trice they trussed up all the pirates and tied them in a great big bundle. All Patagonia Clatterbottom could do was spit and growl like a cornered cat.

"You cheated!" she hissed at Boris. "And you've got a sardine up your nose. That's very fishy if you ask me."

"Yah boo sucks to you," sneered Boris.

5. Little Flo's Good Idea

On board ship, Little Flo had been watching all the action through a telescope.

"Oh dear," she said, when she saw the Woppagobs leap up and grab the pirates.

"We must rescue them," said Ziggy at once.

"We don't have a rowing boat,"

Smudge pointed out. "We can't swim that far."

"We won't have to," laughed Corkella. "We can get a ride from my friends."

Corkella leaned over the ship's side and whistled. Almost immediately several dolphins poked their heads out of the water.

"Can you take us to Woppagob

Island?" she asked, and the dolphins squeaked and nodded.

The pirate children thought this was brilliant and jumped overboard at once. Then they held on to the dolphins tightly as they sped to shore.

It was Little Flo who actually came up with a rescue plan. She whispered in Ziggy's ear.

"It might not work," she added shyly.

"It's worth a try, Little Flo," said Ziggy admiringly.

"You might get hurt," she said, turning pale.

"I might not," grinned Ziggy. But he was only grinning on the outside. Inside, his heart was going boom-de-boom-de-boom.

Ziggy got down on his belly and wriggled towards the Woppagob gang. They were dancing round a big bonfire, singing to celebrate their famous victory.

"We are the Woppagobs,
The Woppagobs are we;
We have caught the pirates,
Hee hee hee hee hee!"

43

It wasn't their best song but they
had made it up on the spot. They were
very pleased with it because it made
Patagonia squirm with rage.

Ziggy hid behind a rock. He could
almost reach out and touch the
Woppagobs. Ziggy took a deep breath.
PYOINNGGG!

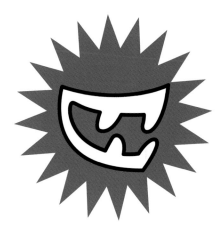

His giant joke teeth shot from his mouth and fastened themselves to Boris Bigbelly's bottom.

"Yowie zowie!" cried Boris, turning on Two-Tooth Charlie. "You just bit me!"

"Did not!" snapped Charlie, completely mystified.

"Did so! You bit my bottie!" Boris aimed a big kick at Charlie's rear, missed and kicked Fifi Foh-Fum instead.

"Kick me, would you? You fish-nosed flab-bag!" She hurled herself at Boris and they were soon rolling across the ground. Charlie and Lily seemed to think it must be some kind of tag wrestling match and joined in.

While the Woppagobs were going at each other hammer and tongs, the children crept up to the teachers and untied them.

6. Patagonia Says, "Thank You." (Fat Chance!)

They all raced down to the shore. "How are we going to get back to the ship?" demanded Patagonia. "You sank our boat, you stupid pimplepots."

"We're NOT stupid pimplepots!" cried Little Flo. "We rescued you and now I wish we hadn't. Ziggy might have been . . . hurt!" she said, swallowing a little sob.

"Come on, you lot," yelled Corkella.
"The dolphins are waiting!"

"Dolphins? I'm not riding on a
fish!" squawked Patagonia. But she
soon jumped on board when she saw
the Woppagobs chasing down the hill
after them.

"They're mammals," Ziggy reminded her as they headed for the ship.

"Fish," insisted Patagonia and immediately found herself tossed into the ocean. A dolphin came up beneath her and lifted her out.

"Glug-glug, FISH," she repeated, and was immediately tossed back into the water. "Splutter-glug-splutter. Oh, fanglefums! All right, mammals!"

Safely back on board, they put on
dry clothes and hung their wet ones
out to dry. Patagonia leaned over the
side of the ship and fed the dolphins
with the last of the sardines that she
had managed to get back from the
Woppagobs.

"That was a brilliant victory," she
crowed. "We beat those Woppagobs,
good and proper."

The children stared at her in
amazement. Patagonia and all the staff
had been captured and tied up. They
had had to be rescued. How was that a
famous victory?

The head teacher eyed Ziggy and Corkella.

"Those dolphins are very clever," she said. "If it wasn't for them, I don't know what would have happened. I trained them personally. They understand everything I say. As for you children, you were utterly useless. Huh!"

She turned her back on them.

The children were outraged.

Was that all the thanks they got? Little
Flo nudged Ziggy. "I found these
before we left the island," she smiled,
and handed him his joke teeth.

Ziggy grinned, took aim and a
moment later there was a startled and
very angry cry.

"Aaaaaaargh!"

I'm splinking my tagglepins!